SILDA
THE ELECTRIC EEL

DEEP DIVE

DEEP DIVE

SILDA
THE ELECTRIC EEL

ADAM BLADE

SCHOLASTIC INC.

ISBN 978-0-545-42768-5

Deep Dive series created by Beast Quest Ltd., London.

Published by Scholastic Inc., 557 Broadway, New York, NY 10012, by arrangement with Working Partners Ltd. SCHOLASTIC and associated logos are trademarks and/or registered trademarks of Scholastic Inc.

12 11 10 9 8 7 6 5 4 3 2 1   12 13 14 15 16 17/0

Designed by Nina Goffi
Printed in the U.S.A.   40
First printing, November 2012

With special thanks to Michael Ford

For Lucas Allan

RULES OF THE SEA 1

LIA SHOT AHEAD ON HER PET SWORDFISH, SPIKE, trailing bubbles after them. The swordfish did a 360-degree spin, showing off. Max gunned the aquabike's engines with a turn of his wrist and roared after her.

"Keep up, Riv!" he called back.

His robodog was nosing through a school of fish. He wagged his metal tail at Max's voice. "Crab, Max! Crab!" he barked.

"Not now," Max said.

Rivet lifted his head, and his leg propellers whirred as he zoomed toward them. Rivet wasn't the *very* latest technology when it came to dogbots, but Max's modifications had made him one of the fastest.

Lia dipped Spike's nose, and the swordfish cut through the water toward the seabed, darting around barnacle-covered boulders.

Anything you can do . . . thought Max, leaning with his body to follow her. He'd always dreamed of owning an aquabike, and this was a Lightning X4. *One of the best!* he thought.

Spike thumped his tail into the seabed, throwing up a cloud of sand. As Max pulled back on the bike's handlebars to climb above it, he gently squeezed the brakes and looked over his shoulder for one last glimpse of Sumara.

Yep, I'm definitely not dreaming, he thought. *That place is real.* The great coral columns of the Merryn city rose through the water, shaped into towers and buildings. Stone walkways stretched between them, and colorful flags of seaweed fluttered in the currents. Glowing plants lit up the underwater streets like torches. Max shook his head in wonder. He couldn't think of anything less like the metal skyscrapers of Aquora. Until yesterday, that island city had been his home.

So much had changed in a single day.

Max had spent his whole life above the water. His dad hated the sea — feared it, even — ever since his wife, Max's mom, had vanished with her brother while exploring. Dad told him that before Max's mom set out, people had made fun of her. They said she was crazy for searching out the Merryn — a legendary underwater people. But she'd been right all along. Max had found that out for himself.

Still, Max would rather she had been wrong, if it meant he could have her back.

His mom's sub, the *Leaping Dolphin*, had never been recovered after it had gone missing. He'd found a scrap of it in the Merryn city of Sumara, but he still had no idea what had happened to her or her brother.

I won't lose my dad as well, he thought.

He felt a squirm in his stomach. His father, Callum North, Chief Defense Engineer of Aquora, had been kidnapped by an evil scientist known to the Merryn people only as "the Professor." He could control the great creatures of the sea with advanced technology. Max didn't know why the Professor had snatched his dad, but he wasn't going to stop searching the oceans until he'd found him again.

The Professor was no friend to the Merryn, either. He had stolen their most treasured possession, the Skull of Thallos, which gave them the power to control the sea. So far, Max and Lia had recovered one part of the skull, but there were three other sections to rescue. Without the skull, the Merryn's aqua powers had been weakened. They couldn't do battle with the Professor's Robobeasts themselves, so Max had agreed to help them.

Max set his jaw as he stared back at the beautiful city. *They need me,* he thought. *And I won't return until the Skull of Thallos is complete.*

Max lifted his hand to the scars on his neck. The new gills still felt strange, but breathing through them was as natural as . . . well, breathing. His skin, which should have wrinkled like he'd spent too long in the bath, was smooth as silk. All thanks to receiving the mysterious Merryn touch!

Rivet arrived at his side, red eyes flashing. "Race, Max!"

"Oh, you think you can beat me, do you?" he replied.

Rivet barked and his tail wagged faster, then he streaked off toward a clump of tall, swaying weeds.

Max tipped the handlebars and shot after him. A host of crabs scuttled out of his way as he wove between the tendrils of seaweed. Ahead of him, a squid pulsed out of sight behind some sharp-looking rocks, and turned an angry orange color. Max was gaining on Rivet, and twisted the throttle to full speed.

"Almost got you . . ." he muttered.

A shape swept in front of him, causing him to brake hard. Max somersaulted over the handlebars. Would the jagged rocks tear the flesh from his back? Thankfully, he bounced over them and onto soft sand, though he was dizzy and confused. He turned and saw Lia sitting on top of Spike, her hands on her hips.

"What in all the seven seas do you think you're doing?" she snapped.

Even underwater, Max felt a blush rise to his cheeks. "I was just —"

"Terrifying innocent creatures?" Lia said.

"Sorry," said Max sheepishly. "It's all so new to me."

Lia's face softened. "This isn't a Breather playground," she said. "We need some ground rules."

"Don't you mean water rules?" Max said.

Lia didn't smile at the joke. "Number One: Respect the ocean. Don't cause damage, and don't harm the creatures that live here. Number Two: The ocean might be beautiful, but it holds many dangers — so be careful around every plant and creature, however innocent they look. And Number Three: Never, ever go into the undertow."

"What's the undertow?" asked Max. He'd just seen Rivet digging in the seabed with his nose. *No bones in there, boy,* he thought.

"You Breathers don't know much, do you?" said Lia. "An undertow is an extremely fast current flowing near the seabed. It's almost invisible, but if you get caught in one, it can be deadly. Are you listening?"

Max's attention snapped back. "What's that? Oh, yes . . . One: Respect. Two: Dangers. Three . . . er . . . What was three?"

"Undertow," Lia said.

"Got it," Max muttered. Rivet was pulling a sparkling pearly shell out of the sand.

"Now, I'm hungry," said Lia, taking off her netted knapsack and feeling inside. She pulled out a disk-shaped green object, broke it in two, and offered half to Max.

"What is it?" he said.

"Seaweed cake," she replied, taking a bite. "Delicious!"

Max brought the cake to his lips and took a nibble. It tasted like salty cardboard. "Mmm," he said, but his voice gave him away.

Lia laughed. "You'll get used to it." She fed a piece of the cake to Spike. "Which way are we supposed to be going?"

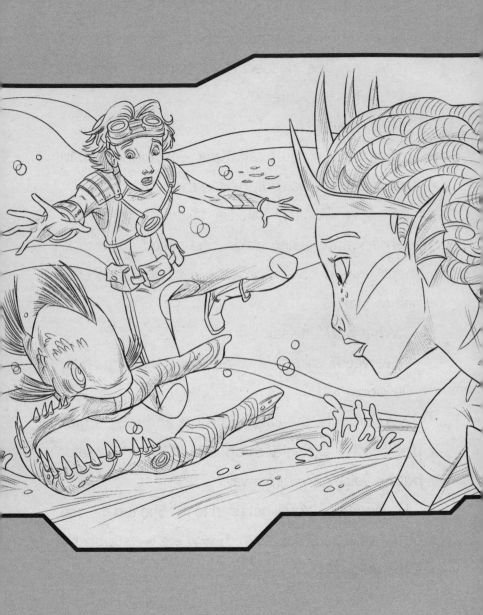

Max called to Rivet. "Here, boy!"

His dogbot dropped the shell and swam over. Max opened the storage compartment in the dog's side and took out the long white jawbone of the Skull of Thallos. The surface glowed, almost translucent.

Max let go of the jawbone, allowing it to float in the water. It slowly rotated, as if guided by invisible currents, until it pointed off to the left. "It worked!" he said. "We'll find the next piece, no problem."

He reached out to take the jawbone when — whoosh! — a large silver fish swooped in from nowhere and snatched the white piece. It darted away before Max even had time to gasp.

The jawbone of the Skull of Thallos had been stolen!

UNDERTOW 2

AFTER IT!" LIA SHOUTED, SQUEEZING SPIKE'S flanks and zipping away.

Max leaped up onto his aquabike and twisted the throttle. The handlebars almost yanked his arms from their sockets as his body was pushed back by the force of the machine's speed.

He drew level with Lia, her silver hair billowing behind her. The fish glinted as it darted through the water ahead. They burst through a group of tiny purple jellyfish, then dipped into an underwater trench filled with prowling manta rays. The thief wasn't giving up. With a flick of its tail, it shot right, and Max almost lost control of the bike as he steered sharply. He couldn't let the fish get away now! Who knew where Rivet was? It didn't matter. He was definitely gaining.

The fish was heading straight for a shimmering patch of water. Max leaned forward in the saddle, reaching out a hand to grab its tail. Behind him, he heard Lia shout something.

"What is it?" he called back.

"Undertow!" she yelled.

Too late! The fish jerked left into the strange rippling current, and a split second later Max followed suit. The force of the water slammed Max and the bike sideways like a massive fist. The bike's engine groaned and squealed as he fought to right it, but he had no chance in the grip of the undertow. It threw him off the saddle, so he was only holding on to the handlebars with one fist, knuckles white. His other arm flailed in the water and it was suddenly hard to draw water into his gills. He felt like he was suffocating.

Boulders and sea shrubs streaked past on either side as the underwater torrent sucked him along, bouncing him off the seabed. Max caught flashes of the silver fish, also swept up in the undertow, but always just ahead of him. He saw Rivet, too, barking madly and tumbling over and over in a tangle of useless leg propellers, waving paws, and a flicking tail.

At least we're in this together! thought Max. But he couldn't get a breath, and his lungs felt crushed. This would be a terrible way to die. Had he been given the Merryn touch only to drown?

Black spots began to crowd the edges of his vision.

There'd be no one to stop the Professor.

Sorry, Dad, he thought. *I've let you down. . . .*

A hand grabbed his arm. Through streaming bubbles he saw Lia's face, her teeth gritted as she yanked him toward her. Next thing he knew he was moving sideways, and the rushing in his ears was gone. As his vision cleared, he saw strands of seaweed floating down from above his head, a topsy-turvy fish swimming past. It took him a moment to understand, but . . . the ocean floor was above his head! He was floating upside down.

"I feel sick," he murmured.

Lia grabbed both arms and spun him around. She floated in front of him.

"Get your bearings," she ordered. "Concentrate! It's important. You don't want to die down here, do you?"

Max's head ached, but he shook it clear. He looked around and saw the channel of the undertow rippling past like a heat haze. They were in a small, shallow crater, with rising shelves of ocean floor on each side. The aquabike rested a short distance away, half-buried in sand like some sort of high-tech shipwreck.

"What about Rivet?" he said.

A series of short barks made him turn. Spike was swimming over the ridge away from the undertow, Rivet gripping a dorsal fin with his front paws. Spike twisted in the water and cast off the dogbot, then gave him a whack on the behind with his powerful tail. Rivet swam in jerky movements toward them. His eyes were facing in different directions, but his tail was wagging. Max banged a fist on the dogbot's head and the eyes swiveled back into place.

"Fun, Max!" Rivet barked. "Again!"

"I don't think so, Riv," he said. "That was close." He turned to Lia. "You were amazing. Thank —"

The Merryn stabbed a webbed finger at Max's chest. "Didn't I tell you?" she said. "Rule Number Three! How short are Breather memories?"

"I know, I'm sorry," said Max, "but you didn't actually tell me what an undertow looked like."

"I can't believe I went after you!" said Lia, smacking her forehead. "Count yourself lucky, Max. Next time might be different."

Max felt guilt settle in his stomach. She was really upset, and all because he couldn't remember three simple rules. "I'm sorry," he said. "And thank you. I mean it. You saved my life."

"For the second time."

"For the second time, yes," said Max. "Come on, I'm not going to kiss your foot-fins."

Lia rolled her eyes. "Breathers!" she muttered.

Max swam over to his aquabike. Straining against the seabed, he pulled it loose and checked the controls. Thankfully it didn't seem damaged, other than

a cracked screen over the depth gauge. He could fix it easily enough when they had a chance to rest.

"We lost the jawbone," said Lia, gazing at the empty space where the fish had swum off. She looked as though she was about to cry. "I've let my dad down."

Max realized the Quest meant as much to her as it did to him. Her dad was the Merryn king, and he'd put his trust in both of them. Spike rolled onto his side and nuzzled up to Lia.

"We might be able to find the fish again if we follow the undertow," said Max. "Or it might drop the jawbone when it realizes it can't eat it." He turned on the bike's thrusters and climbed toward the edge of the crater. "Wow!" he gasped as he reached the top. "Come and check this out!"

Lia guided Spike toward him, and together they rose over the lip of the crater into warm and gentle currents. Lia gasped, too. The water ahead was almost sky blue, filled with plants and fish more colorful than Max had ever seen. There were scarlet sea snakes fluttering through the water, and lobsters with green eyes on stalks, picking their way across the ocean bed. Looming over all of it was a vast wall of white coral, glistening with sparkling points like a million diamonds. It rose from the seafloor up as high as Max could see. "What is this place?" he asked.

"I don't know," said Lia, "but it's beautiful!"

Rivet suddenly shot through the water between them and hurled himself headlong into a carpet of black seaweed. The thick, dark plants writhed, and drifts of sand rose above the dogbot's wagging tail. When he emerged, he was holding the silver fish in his jaws. And in the fish's mouth was . . .

"The jawbone of Thallos!" Lia gasped.

"The fish was just hiding. Well done, Rivet!" Max cried.

He looked at Lia, and saw that she was beaming the biggest, whitest smile. Rivet swam toward them with the fish squirming in his mouth. The fish had ragged, sharp teeth, and Max wasn't looking forward to prying out the jawbone. But as soon as he touched the Skull of Thallos, the fish released it without a fight.

"Weird!" said Lia. "It's almost like the skull controlled the fish."

"Better let this catch go," Max said to the dogbot.

Rivet whined, but opened his mouth. The fish streaked off, panicked but unhurt.

Max let the jawbone float in the water. It glowed a faint blue and tipped to point upward toward the looming white cliff.

"Looks like we go that way," said Lia.

"I don't understand," said Max. "Why did the fish stop here?"

"Maybe the power of the skull was guiding it," said Lia, shrugging. "It wasn't hiding very well, was it? Not if Rivet could find it. Maybe the skull brought it here. And if so, maybe the next piece is nearby."

Max shivered, even though the water was warm. If the second piece of the skull was close, then so was a Robobeast. He looked at his three companions. Cephalox the Cyber Squid had almost defeated them. *Are we ready to face the Professor again?*

SNAPPERFISH 3

AS THEY STARED AT THE LOOMING WHITE CORAL, Max pressed the green button behind Rivet's ear and the dogbot's back compartment slid open. Max slotted the piece of the jawbone inside and closed the panel. "Keep it safe, boy," he said.

Rivet gave an electronic whimper. "Scared, Max."

"I know," said Max. "Me, too."

"Let's go," said Lia.

Spike rose upward, eyes alert, with the Merryn girl clutching his fin. Max rode his aquabike beside them. Up close, he saw that the coral cliffs weren't as smooth and solid as they'd looked. The coral grew in swirls and branches, patterns that made Max's eyes blur. There were thousands of holes in the wall, leading deeper into the coral. Tiny fish swam around the openings, darting in and out. Here and there patches of weeds clung to the wall. Max saw a chameleon fish flatten itself against the white, its scales fading from brown to white so that, in the blink of an eye, Max could no longer tell where it was. Sparkling points shone like polished crystals. The stone seemed almost warm and alive. Max reached out to lay his hand against it.

"Don't," said Lia.

Max felt a sharp pain in his palm. "Ouch!"

He snatched back his hand and saw a trail of blood clouding out from a cut.

Lia sighed through her gills and turned Spike around to face him. "What was Rule Number Two?" she asked.

Max tried to remember.

Lia raised her eyebrows and Spike blew a chain of bubbles. "The ocean is full of dangers," she said. "Everything can be a threat. Stay alert, Max."

She climbed off Spike and swam close to the rock face. She broke off several wide strands of gray seaweed. "Hold out your hand."

Max did as he was told, and Lia placed the weeds around his palm. It stuck to his skin like melted wax. "It's called clotleaf," she said, stuffing the remaining strands in her knapsack. "It'll seal up your wound."

"Thanks," said Max.

Rivet barked and did a full turn in the water as if he was chasing his tail. "Danger, Max!"

"Looks like Rivet's got a problem," said Max. "That undertow must have loosened his screws."

Lia's head jerked around and her nose twitched as

she sniffed the water. She glanced down and her eyes widened. "There's nothing wrong with Rivet," she said. "We need to go — quickly!"

"Why?" Max turned in the water, but he couldn't see anything.

Lia pointed downward with a webbed hand.

Now Max saw them. Three dark shapes drifting through the water below. He swallowed.

"Snapperfish," said Lia. "Come on."

Max twisted the bike's throttle and they shot upward. Rivet tucked his forelegs up to his body and his rear propellers whizzed at full speed.

"What are snapperfish?" Max shouted over the bike's engine.

"Ferocious sea predators," Lia replied. "They can detect blood from miles away. They must have smelled your hand."

Max turned back and saw the fish darting upward, yellow, wide-spaced eyes gleaming over long jaws. Their eyes were fixed on *him*.

"They're gaining!" he shouted.

Lia, just ahead, steered closer to the coral, threading in and out of the jutting shards. "Hardly anything can outswim a snapper in the open water," she called back. "Look for a way through the coral!"

But all the openings were too small.

Max glanced back over his shoulder. For a moment, he thought they'd escaped their pursuers, but then two snapperfish rounded a coral outcrop. He watched them regroup and steer toward him.

"We've lost one!" he said.

"No, we haven't," said Lia. "They work as a team — it'll come from above."

Spike nosed in and out of cracks, searching for an escape route. As Rivet buzzed alongside them, Max had an idea. "Hold still, boy!" he said, leaning across with one hand and keeping the bike straight with the other. He opened the compartment on Rivet's back and took out the jawbone.

This had better work, he thought. He was going to put all his faith in the mysterious strength of the Skull of Thallos.

At once, the jawbone tugged him to the left. Max let the bike steer in that direction, too.

"Where are you going?" called Lia.

"This way!" he replied.

The jawbone guided him toward what looked like a patch of thick scarlet weeds coating the coral shelf. The tugging sensation stopped. Max reached gingerly into the weeds and pushed them apart. Peering through, he saw black space beyond. A passageway! Just as he'd thought — the skull had helped them. It was almost as though it understood their danger. But would the space be big enough?

Max stowed the jawbone and got to work clearing the slimy weeds from the opening. Rivet helped, too, tearing whole patches off the rock with his jaws. Lia grabbed a handful and looked over her shoulder, her face pale. "Quicker!" she said. "They're coming."

As Max ripped out more weeds, he saw a hole as wide as one of the drain covers in Aquora City. "You'll have to leave the bike," said Lia.

Max nodded and reached for the aquabike. He tugged open the storage compartment and began hunting for his infrared goggles. "You go first."

With a kick of her feet, Lia slipped through the gap. Spike backed off, gesturing to the hole with his sword. "You next!" Lia called. Max saw the yellow gleam of eyes coming toward him as he secured the goggles to his belt. The lead snapperfish was at least as big as he was.

Max pulled himself through the opening, feeling the coral cut into his fingers. He wriggled along the passage, the coral scratching against his sides. Lia's hand grabbed his and tugged him the rest of the way. Rivet shot through next, barking madly, and Spike came last of all.

Max found himself in a huge white cavern that glistened on all sides. The water was cold and gloomy,

with shifting clouds of plankton hanging in the still-
ness. Beyond he saw the opening to another, larger
tunnel. Lia looked back from near the tunnel opening. "Get away, quickly!" she cried to Max.

He pushed himself through the water, legs kicking
hard, and twisted around to see the first snapperfish pushing through the passage, shaking its body
from side to side and gnashing its jaws. There wasn't
any time to block it.

The predator burst into the cavern, followed by its
two friends. Their muscular gray bodies were lined
with scars and stubby fins. Six hungry yellow eyes
followed Max and Lia. The snapperfish opened their
jaws to reveal rows of teeth like needles. *They'd tear
my head off in a heartbeat,* Max realized.

Spike burst through the water, shielding Max and
Lia with his body and swishing his nose-sword from
side to side. The snapperfish watched him, their ugly
bodies still.

Spike darted right toward the center of the group. The snapperfish scattered, then countered. One clamped its teeth over Spike's tail, and another grabbed his jutting sword. Spike writhed, but couldn't shake free. The remaining snapper moved in and his jaws closed over Spike's back.

"No!" shouted Lia. The swordfish twisted in pain.

Max had no weapon. He had left his hyperblade behind, stowed on his aquabike. And if he didn't do something soon, Spike was finished.

SHIPWRECK 4

BUBBLES SPILLED FROM SPIKE'S GILLS AS HE
fought. Rivet barked and leaped into action, butting
one of the fish off with his snout. The snapper was
bigger than anything the dogbot had ever caught,
but at least he could distract it. The snapper wheeled
away, looking for another angle of attack. Rivet struck
again, lowering his head and ramming the top of his

flat metal skull into the side of the fish that was holding Spike. The snapper squealed with pain and relaxed its jaws — just enough for Spike to wriggle free. Now all they had to do was escape. . . .

Max glanced all around. Deeper in the cavern, he noticed a glint of metal. No, not just a glint. His straining eyes followed the line of some sort of vessel. Surely not. Were there people down here?

"Hold on a second," he shouted.

"What?" gasped Lia. "We need you here!"

Max swam down toward the vessel, kicking hard. It was abandoned — a submarine resting at the base of the cavern at an angle, among broken fragments of coral. Weeds grew over the hull. A few small portholes stared out from the side, the glass green with algae. There was a jagged metal tear in the base of the sub. Debris floated within. Max saw a rusty compass, and clothing of some sort. What had happened to the pilots? The submarine type wasn't one Max had seen before. It was old-fashioned and probably built years ago.

He spotted the main entry hatch — the dry hatch — for boarding the sub from a jetty at sea level. There was another hatch on the underside — the wet hatch — which had an airlock for slipping in and out underwater.

Perhaps we can hide inside, Max thought. *Or maybe . . .*

"Lia! Spike! Rivet!" He waved. "Down here — all of you!"

Max yanked a lever, and the dry hatch opened. A cloud of filthy seawater flooded over him. He slipped down through the open hatch. Lia and Rivet sped toward Max and followed him into the sub. Spike came last of all, still fighting off one snapper with the other two on his tail. Batting aside floating packages of food and tattered old diving suits, Max led them through the sub's central chamber toward the wet-hatch airlock. He passed a swinging cabinet

door and spied a harpoon gun propped inside. He grabbed it, just in case. He kicked toward the wet hatch. "This way!" he called back.

They piled into the airlock. Spike twisted as he came through last, bashing off the snapperfish. The predator threw itself at them with gaping jaws. Max slammed his palm on the LOCK button and the door swished shut. The snapper slammed its face against the viewing panel, smearing it with black fish drool.

"Bad fish," barked Rivet.

"Yes, bad fish," said Max, patting his dog on the head. "But we're safe for the moment. Good job on rescuing Spike." Behind them was the outer wet-hatch door, leading back into the cavern.

Lia ran her hands over Spike's flank, which trailed blood from teeth wounds. The swordfish's eyes seemed dim and colorless. "Poor thing!" she said. "He saved our lives."

"What about the clotleaf?" said Max.

"Good thinking," said Lia. She took out the weeds and gave a handful to Max. Between them, they laid the makeshift bandages over Spike's wounds and the bleeding ceased at once. Outside, the snap-perfish had stopped bashing themselves against the glass. Rivet cocked his head at Max, as if to say, *What now?*

"I wonder what we should do now," said Lia. "We're in here, and they're out there. As soon as we try to slip out again we're fish food!"

Max looked over the controls and saw the AIR-LOCK RELEASE button. He grinned. "Help me get this panel off."

"Why?"

"It's time to do some rewiring."

He used the tip of the harpoon gun to pry open the panel, then Lia got her fingers under the edge. Feet against the wall, she yanked it free. Beneath the panel was a tangle of different-colored cables over a circuit board.

This was old technology, the sort of stuff Max's dad had taught him when he was just a little boy. He found the right thermoresin cable — red with blue bands — and hooked a finger around it.

"Are you sure you know what you're doing?" asked Lia.

Max smiled. "You might know the names of a thousand species of starfish," he said, "but I know a thing or two about engineering."

The truth was, he wasn't one hundred percent sure he had the right wire. Breaking this circuit would either close the dry hatch, locking the snapperfish in the main chamber of the sub, or it would open the door that was now holding them back.

Life, or death.

He closed his eyes and pulled.

The wire snapped. Through the glass he saw the main entry hatch clamp shut. The snapperfish saw it, too, and darted in panicked circles around the enclosed chamber. "Yes!" Max said. He pressed the WET-HATCH RELEASE button and the outer airlock, leading out into the cavern, swished open.

Lia's jaw dropped. "Wow," she said.

They swam out through the wet hatch. Spike twisted in joy, and Max was glad to see him back to normal.

Rivet swam in front of the hatches, taunting the snapperfish inside. He turned to Max. "Stupid fish! Clever Max!" he barked.

"It's just lucky we found the sub," Max said. "I don't get it, though — why would anyone come down here?"

"Probably looking for precious stones," said Lia, climbing onto Spike's back.

"I wonder why they crashed."

"Breathers might be brave, but they're foolish, too," said Lia. "Rule Number Two, remember? They don't respect the sea."

"I wonder what happened to them," said Max, remembering the scrap of diving suit floating in the sub's chamber. "Do you think they made it back to the surface?"

"I doubt it," said Lia. "The pressure down here is too much for Breathers. They probably drowned and gave the fish a good feast."

Max shivered. His mom's face flashed into his mind, along with the nightmares he used to suffer about her drowning.

"Let's keep going," he said, shaking his head clear of the pictures.

He called Rivet over and took out the jawbone, letting it float in the water. He'd trust the Skull of Thallos with his life, he realized now. It glowed and drifted around to point to the tunnel he'd spotted on the other side of the cavern — deeper into the ancient coral caves.

Max tucked the harpoon gun into Rivet's compartment. Without his aquabike, he swam behind his friends. He took a deep breath as they entered the tunnel that would lead them into the heart of this coral maze.

"All right, Robobeast!" Max muttered. "We're coming to get you!"

LABYRINTH 5

MAX AND LIA SWAM ALONG THE TUNNEL. The only light came from the glowing jawbone.

Rivet switched on his headlamp, and the way ahead lit up in a faint red glow. Fish winked out of sight and hundreds of pink shells reflected light up from the tunnel floor. Yellow weeds brushed at Max's feet.

By the lamplight, Max saw that the way ahead forked. A path on the left led deeper into the glowing coral. Another on the right sloped gently up toward a sparkling cave. "Which way?" he asked.

"We should trust the power of Thallos," Lia replied.

Max held the jawbone loosely, and it twisted in his hand, pointing to the left fork. He was about to swim ahead when he noticed that Lia had stopped. "What is it?"

She stared into the tunnel. "Well, we can follow the skull into the maze, but what about finding our way out again?"

Lia was right. Sinking to the bottom of the tunnel, he fished around for several of the pink shells, then swam back past Lia and into the left tunnel. Every few strokes, he dropped one on the ground.

He'd scattered almost all of them when he realized Lia was laughing.

"What's so funny?" he asked. "Don't you get it? I'm laying down markers so we can find our way back."

"Sorry!" Lia covered her mouth with one webbed hand and pointed at Max's feet with the other. "Look!"

Max peered down. One by one, the pink shells sprouted crab legs and scurried off. "Fine," he said. "But what *can* we use?"

Lia swam to the tunnel floor. She plucked a flower head off one of the yellow weeds. "We call this the sunshine flower," she said. "It only grows from this sort of coral, so it's rare."

Looking closer, Max saw the petals of the flower were actually long pods. "And how's it going to help?" he asked.

Lia squeezed one of the pods between her fingers. It burst open, throwing out a bright yellow ink that hung like a cloud in the water. Rivet barked

with surprise and drifted forward to sniff at the shiny substance.

"Wow!" said Max.

"The pollen lasts for a few hours," said Lia, handing some of the pods to Max. "Let's go."

They pressed on into the eerie darkness, bursting pods to leave markers in the water, and dipping occasionally to pick more sunshine flowers. There were fewer fish here, and soon even the weeds ran out. Max felt odd currents of water pressing around him, like the pulse of a heartbeat. Spike must have sensed it, too, because each time one of the vibrations hit, his nose-sword twitched.

"What is that?" asked Max.

Lia shook her head. "I've never felt anything like it before."

One thing was certain — the shock waves filtering through the tunnel were getting stronger, like a drum beating ever closer. Soon Max realized that the walls themselves had begun to shake. Still the dogbot's lamp picked out nothing ahead but the twisting tunnel.

Max felt the hairs on the back of his neck tingle as the jawbone turned in his hand. It pointed behind them.

"Er . . . Lia," he said. "Whatever that is, I don't think it's coming from ahead."

She stopped and turned. Another blast shuddered past them. Her silver hair fluttered back from her face. "You're right," she whispered. "Let's keep going — if we're going to fight properly, we can't afford to get trapped in here."

They swam faster, and though Max looked back several times, he couldn't see anything. The rumbles grew louder and more frequent, echoing his own heartbeat. There was no doubt about it — something was coming after them.

"Bad, Max," Rivet whimpered, his microphone hushed.

The passage narrowed, then all of a sudden emerged into another cavern. This one was enormous. Max swam closer to one of the walls, and gasped. It was made of metal. Huge sheets beaten into curves and bolted down. It was as if they were inside a giant metal ball!

Lia ran her fingers over the metal. "This wasn't built by Merryn," she whispered.

In Max's hand, the fragment of the Skull of Thallos glowed bright blue. It tugged back toward the tunnel they'd come through.

"There must be another way out," said Max. "We can't go back there."

He stowed the jawbone in Rivet's compartment and led the way down toward the bottom of the cavern, searching for an opening. Even the floor was made of metal, covered in a fine layer of sand. His eyes were still adjusting to the gloom when Rivet's headlamp caught a flash of something. Max made

out the bones of a large skeleton. Then more — the ribs of some creature picked white and clean. Lia was trembling beside him.

"This is a graveyard," she muttered. Max suddenly remembered his infrared goggles and took them from his belt. The cavern floor was littered with the remains of dozens of sea-dwellers. Some looked like they had been human, but some had the fused foot and hand bones of Merryn. There were weapons, too. Harpoons, blasters, even a handheld torpedo launcher. All were rusted or broken.

"It's as if they all came down here to fight something," said Max.

"And lost," added Lia.

Max thought of the empty submarine and shuddered.

A rumble from the tunnel rattled the bones, and the great metal walls shook. "It's almost here," said Max.

Lia swept over the debris and skeletons, and plucked out a lance. "A Merryn hunting spear," she said. "Made of pearl. An ancient weapon, but powerful. My grandfather used one."

Max swam up to face the dark empty mouth of the passage. "Stay behind me," he said. "A harpoon gun will do more to keep them back than an old spear."

With a flick of her foot-fins, Lia was at his side. "We face this together," she said.

Another boom shook the water around them. Lia laid a hand on Spike's side. "Stay brave."

Max patted Rivet's back. "You're a good boy," he said.

The tunnel ahead filled with a shape.

The Robobeast had arrived.

ELECTRIC ENEMY 6

A HEAD EDGED THROUGH THE WATER, ALMOST as wide as the tunnel. The creature's skin was as smooth as a beach pebble, gleaming in the faint light.

Max and Lia backed away.

Two tiny unblinking eyes like dull black marbles watched them.

The Beast's body followed, huge lengths of snaking pale flesh spilling into the cavern.

It's a gigantic eel! Max realized.

As the creature's tail finally slid from the tunnel, the body formed into a tight coil, filling almost half the cavern. Its staring head came to rest over its back and its lipless mouth parted to reveal jagged, close-packed teeth. Max made out a robotic harness behind its neck, just like the one worn by Cephalox the Cyber Squid. Metal clasps and coils of cable sat next to the eel's pale flesh — the mechanism by which the Professor controlled his slave. Mounted on top of the harness, under a glass dome, was the second piece of the Skull of Thallos. Max peered closer — it was an eye socket and a section of cheekbone.

Lia lifted her pearl spear and Max raised his harpoon gun.

"Why isn't it attacking?" he hissed.

With a click and a whir, a panel on the harness slid open. A red orb, like the one Max had seen on Cephalox's tentacle, swiveled around and jerked closer. It blinked like an eye.

"Hello, Max," said a voice, deep and distorted by electronics. "Welcome to the lair of Silda."

"Who are you?" shouted Max, loud enough to disguise his fear.

"You can call me . . . the Professor."

Max felt his stomach jolt at the sound of his enemy's voice. He could see there was no place for the Professor to hide on the eel's body. *He must be controlling it remotely,* thought Max.

"How does the Professor know your name?" whispered Lia.

"I don't —"

"Your father told me you were clever," continued the voice, "but now I'm beginning to doubt that. You walked right into my trap."

Trap?

Max glanced at Lia, then at the metal walls. There was only one way out, and they'd have to get past Silda to reach it.

"Where is my father?" asked Max.

"Safe," said the Professor. "For now. Which is more than I can say for you two. There's no escape from here. Silda's lair will be your grave."

Max raised the harpoon gun. "We'll see about that."

"Ah, my old weapon," said the voice. "That brings back memories."

Of course! thought Max. "The crashed sub belonged to you!" *No wonder there were no bodies in the sub.*

Rivet surged forward on speeding propellers and clamped his jaws over Silda's tail. A crackle of blue lightning shot along the Robobeast's coils and over the dogbot. Rivet's metal body spasmed, his legs quivering, then he drifted away.

Max wanted to go to the dogbot, but he couldn't leave Lia. "Silda's an electric eel!" he said. "Don't get close."

Rivet was making strange noises — buzzes and pings. *Just like back in Aquora when I'd only just built him and I put his circuit board in the wrong way,* thought Max.

Now he understood the metal walls. If Silda touched them, they would become electrified. There was no way out, and fighting the Professor's creature was going to be even more difficult than Max had thought.

Silda uncoiled slowly and nosed through the water after the stunned dogbot. The Robobeast opened its mouth.

"No!" shouted Max, swimming between the gaping jaws and his dogbot. He aimed the gun and fired, launching the harpoon. Silda slunk to one side as the missile cut through the water, a wire snaking out behind it. The barbed point punctured the eel's side, and a blue pulse shot back up the wire and into Max's arm. It felt like something had grabbed his spine and snatched him through the water. His hand clamped on to the gun as the current zapped through him.

Max couldn't feel a thing. He saw his limbs sprawled in the water, but when he tried to move them, he couldn't. Slowly, his skin began to tingle all over with pins and needles. The harpoon gun drifted through the water, out of reach. *Great. Now I haven't even got a weapon,* he thought.

"Are you all right?" asked Lia, arriving at his side.

Max managed to nod. Lia tugged him away from the eel's mouth.

"I thought you were dead!" she said.

"So did I," said Max.

Thankfully, Rivet seemed to have recovered. He was barking angrily in front of the eel's head, retreating just out of reach.

Max struggled upright in the water. "We have to get that harness off," he said. "That's how the Professor is controlling the Robobeast."

But as he pointed at the harness, he saw more blue splinters of light crackling across it. *There's no way I'm touching that,* he thought.

"How are we supposed to deactivate the harness if we can't even touch it?" asked Lia.

The red camera eye rotated to face them.

"Uh-oh," said Max.

Out of the corner of his eye, he saw the eel's slab of a tail arcing through the water. Barely stopping to think, he pushed Lia backward. She gave a squeak of surprise as she tumbled clear, and the tail smacked into him. Electricity surged through his limbs. It felt like his skeleton was being ripped out of him as he spun through the water toward the outer wall. Then he slammed into the metal and another shock vibrated across his skin.

Max drifted in the water, every nerve on fire, unable to move.

I was lucky with the first Robobeast, he thought, *but this one's going to be the end of me. . . .*

Silda's huge head rose through the water to face him. The eel's mouth parted in what looked like a horrible smile.

"Met your match this time, haven't you?" said the Professor. "I bet you wish you'd stayed in Aquora now."

KILLER COILS 7

LEAVE HIM ALONE!" SHOUTED LIA. MAX MANaged to turn his head and saw his Merryn friend on top of Spike. She clutched the pearl spear.

"I don't take orders from fish," said the Professor.

Silda's jaws opened wide and Max stared past the needle teeth and into the black throat. He hoped death would be quick.

Then the eel's head jerked sideways.

"What — ?" gasped the Professor. "How did — ?"

Still too weak to move, Max saw the pearl spear jutting from Silda's flank. The red eye darted this way and that, trying to see what was happening. *Of course!* thought Max. *Lia's spear's not made of metal, so it can't conduct electricity.* The eel's body writhed and wriggled. At last the beady black eyes spotted the spear. Silda's jaws snatched it, yanked it free, and tossed it across the cave.

The Robobeast's head flashed around to face Lia and her swordfish. She tried to swim away, but Silda moved quickly, blocking her route with a huge coil. Max watched, willing his body to move, as the Beast slowly surrounded Lia with its long, muscular body. She darted back and forth, unable to escape and unable to touch the electric eel's deadly flesh.

But why isn't Silda closing in for the kill? Max thought foggily. It could shock her at any time.

Sensation was returning to Max's body, but he knew he couldn't swim anywhere yet. His arms and legs felt like jelly.

The harness on Silda's neck swished open again, and another robotic arm extended in Lia's direction. Attached to the end of it was a chain saw with jagged metal teeth.

"I haven't gutted a fish for quite some time," said the Professor. "This should be fun."

The saw began to spin, until its whizzing blades became a blur. Lia screamed.

Max shook himself. He had to move. He couldn't let his friend die. She'd saved his life. What had he done for her, apart from lead her into this deadly trap? The metal arm extended over Silda's head and whirled straight toward Lia.

Move, legs! Max willed.

His left foot twitched, a warm feeling flooding in. Then his right foot.

Move, arms!

He managed to cup his hands and pull himself through the water.

Silda's coils shifted to let the chain saw pass and Lia screamed louder.

Max swam closer, feeling stronger by the second. He saw a gap had opened up in the moving coils. Lia hadn't spotted it — her eyes were fixed on the buzzing saw.

Max reached the gap. The eel's slimy skin crackled with power. He saw Lia's foot on the other side and reached through. The saw buzzed beside her head and she cowered back, closing her eyes.

Max seized her ankle and yanked, kicking with his legs at the same time. Lia shot through the gap with Spike in tow, just as the saw descended. It bit into the metal wall, showering blue sparks and filling Max's ears with a horrible grinding squeal.

Lia opened her eyes and saw him. "How did you — ?"

"That's not important," he interrupted. "Where's your spear?"

Lia spun around, then pointed to the cavern floor. "There!"

Max saw it, too. "Rivet!" he yelled. "Fetch!"

The dogbot darted down into the depths. As he carried the spear up to Max, Silda was pulling the saw teeth free of the cavern wall. They'd chewed an ugly gash in the metal.

"The spear's the only thing that can touch Silda," said Max.

"But it barely gave it a pinprick last time."

Max took the spear from Rivet's mouth. It was as light as driftwood. "I'm not going to stab the Beast with it. I've got a better idea."

The electric eel's head snapped toward them. "Split up," shouted Lia.

As the Robobeast shot toward them, chain saw buzzing angrily, they each swam in opposite directions. Silda went for the nearest target — Rivet. The

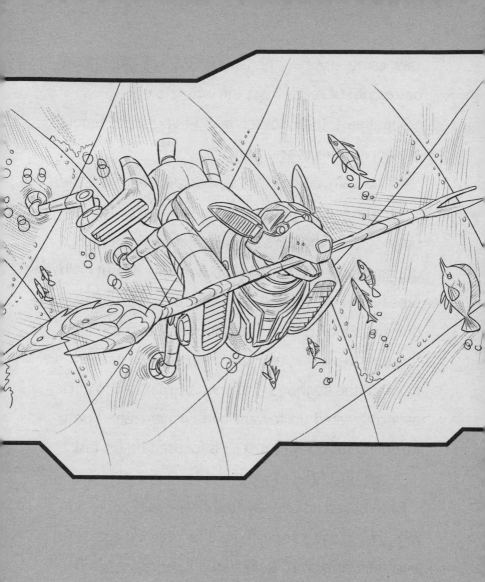

saw came close to his snout. With a yelp, Rivet darted out of reach, past the writhing coils.

The Beast tried to follow, getting in a tangle among its own snaking tail.

Max swam up to Silda's neck and rammed the spear into the harness's latches. He planted his rubber boots on the eel's slippery hide, trying to get a grip and working the spear back and forth. But each time he got the spear point into position, Silda's wild bucking shook it free. The Robobeast pursued Rivet through the water, and the chain saw whizzed ever closer to the dogbot's wagging tail. Max had to duck as a coil reared up toward him. Water rushed past, buffeting his body, but still he focused on his task.

"Look out!" called Lia.

Max looked up and saw the cavern wall approaching. If he didn't jump off, he'd be crushed against it and fried to a crisp. *But if I don't get rid of this harness, Rivet's going to be cut in two!*

He lodged the spear under the harness's catch and swung his legs up against the wall. His rubber soles thumped into the metal. Max strained, locking his legs, but Silda was pushing him. His knees buckled as he tried to keep his body from touching the wall. He gripped the spear and worked it harder into the harness's fastenings. His thighs burned. He could see now that the Professor had forgotten about Rivet. All his energy was focused on finishing off Max, crushing him or electrocuting him. Or both.

The strength in his legs was fading and still the harness didn't budge.

I'm going to die down here, just like Mom. And so will Dad.

Max had nothing left. He closed his eyes, gritted his teeth, and waited for the terrible shock to come.

THE BLACK CAVES 8

*C*LICK.

The pressure eased and Max opened his eyes.

He still gripped the spear, but the metal catches were open and the harness had fallen away from Silda's body, fizzing with sparks.

"No!" screeched the Professor's voice. "No, no,

no! It can't be. . . . Attack them! Kill . . ." The cries died to an electronic whine, then nothing.

The giant eel turned its head to watch the robotic equipment drift to the bottom of the metal cavern.

I did it! Max thought, pushing off from the wall.

Silda nosed through the water until its head was close to Max. He held the spear loosely, just in case, but something told him the electric eel wasn't a threat any longer. Its black eyes looked shining and alive now, full of intelligence and kindness. "You're not that fierce at all, are you?" he said, lowering the spear.

After two slow blinks, the eel's body twitched and darted away through the water, free of the Professor's control. Max felt the tug of its wake as the powerful coils shot past. Without looking back, Silda entered the tunnel and disappeared into the maze.

Rivet's playful barking drew Max's attention back to the cavern. The dogbot was sniffing at the discarded harness, tugging at something with his teeth.

"The next piece of the Skull of Thallos!" said Lia, scooting past on Spike. Max took her outstretched arm and felt himself being pulled through the water.

They slowed to a halt beside Rivet, and Max helped the dogbot pry the fragment of bone from the harness. It was the top part of the skull — an oval-shaped eye socket, wide enough to put his hand through, above a heavy ridge of bone. He held it in his hands, feeling the strange power pulsing from its surface. Lia punched him lightly on the arm.

"So Merryn weapons are completely useless, are they?" she said.

"Only if you don't know how to use them," said Max, grinning.

Lia punched him again. *A bit harder this time,* he thought.

He stowed the piece of the skull in Rivet's body compartment, and together they swam back up toward the tunnel.

"We should rest awhile," said Lia. "We've had a few shocks."

"You could say that," Max replied.

But curiosity gnawed at him. "I want to check out the Professor's sub wreck first," he said. "There might be some clues to where he's keeping my dad."

The Merryn girl nodded. "Good thinking. Let's take a look."

The clouds of yellow ink from the sunshine flowers still hung in the water to guide them. Max held on to Rivet's tail as the four friends raced through the twisting tunnels. At last they emerged into the cavern with the crippled craft resting on the seabed. When they reached it, Max could see the snapper-fish still darting madly around inside. From the debris drifting around in the sub's hull, it looked like they'd chewed up most of what was left.

He smacked his hand against the porthole. "No! If there were any clues, they've been torn apart now."

Lia put a hand on his shoulder. "Maybe not. There might be something left."

A snapperfish drifted past the porthole, watching them.

"Even if there is," said Max, "we can't get inside. Those fish are madder than ever!"

Lia tapped her foot-fins on the side of the sub. "Maybe we can't *all* go inside, but Rivet can. He's metal."

The dogbot backed away with a whine. "Not inside, Max!" he barked. His tail curled between his leg propellers.

Max beckoned Rivet toward him. "On your back, boy."

Rivet rolled over slowly. Max unfastened the dog's belly hatch, exposing several wires and waterproof circuit boards. "I know how we can keep those snappers at bay."

He swapped over a few fiber-optic wires and deactivated one of the circuits, then snapped the hatch closed. "Now," he said as Rivet turned upright, "I need you to get the sub's CPU."

Rivet nodded and gave a short bark.

"What have you done to him?" asked Lia.

"You'll see," said Max, opening the wet hatch.

"And what's a CPU?" said Lia.

"Just watch," said Max.

Rivet kicked his way in. Max sealed the hatch and Rivet pressed the inner AIRLOCK DOOR ENTRY button with his paw. It opened and Rivet swam into the main chamber of the vessel. The snapperfish darted at him, jaws wide. But as the first one hit, blue sparks shot off Rivet's body and along the fish's scales. The snapperfish squirmed away. More blue crackles sent the other two fleeing as well.

"You electrified him!" said Lia.

Max grinned. "That's right. Just like Silda. I reversed a couple circuits and switched off the insulators. Just don't pet him until I've switched him back."

Lia giggled, and through the porthole they watched Rivet pass across the central control console. The dogbot grabbed hold of a metal slab attached to the wall, and tore it off with his teeth.

"All ships have a CPU," said Max. "It stands for 'Central Processing Unit.' It's the sub's main computer, and it contains all the most important information."

"Not bad, for Breathers," said Lia. "Let's hope it can tell us what the Professor's up to."

And where my dad is, thought Max.

The snapperfish didn't try to follow Rivet back into the airlock. They'd learned their lesson and were staying way back on the far side of the sub. When Rivet emerged, he rolled over to let Max change back the wires. Max patted him on the head. "Good work, boy."

Rivet dropped the CPU into his hands. Max powered it up, and a red bar flashed on its side.

"Power's down," said Max. "Those snapperfish must have damaged it. Or it's just very old." Feeling unsure, he switched it on.

A green screen lit up on the front of the box, showing a crackling image that drifted in and out of focus.

"Water damage?" Lia asked.

Max shook his head. "Snapperfish. One of them must have bashed into it." He began scrolling through the data. It was mostly about engineering and navigation. "Boring . . . boring . . ." he muttered. "Hang on. What's this?"

He had found a few lines of code, hidden in a file about water-pressure monitoring. He opened it, and an image blinked up, showing what looked like a map of roads. It rotated in three dimensions, and Max realized they weren't roads at all, but a network of passageways and larger open areas. The lettering at the bottom of the screen read THE BLACK CAVES.

"I've never heard of them," said Lia, leaning over his shoulder.

Max pressed a pad on the CPU, to skip to the next image. The projection faded to black. He pressed the pad again, but nothing happened. He switched it off, then on again. Nothing.

"It died!" he said. He shook it, but it didn't do any good.

"Maybe those caves are where the Professor is keeping your father," said Lia hopefully.

Max let the CPU drop among the broken fragments of coral.

"Maybe," he said. "Either way, it's the only clue we've got."

INSIDE THE SHELL 9

RIVET NUZZLED AT MAX'S ARM.

"You have to be strong, Max," said Lia. "If we follow the Professor, we'll find your father." She reached into her knapsack. "Here, this'll make you feel better."

She pulled out a piece of seaweed cake and offered it to him.

Max smiled. "It wouldn't be my first choice, but thanks."

They swam across to a boulder at the side of the cavern and sat side by side. Max bit off a chunk of the cake and chewed thoughtfully. The Professor was an evil man, but he wasn't stupid. He didn't simply kill for the sake of it, and as long as Max's ·father was useful to him, he'd be safe.

I just have to find him before his usefulness runs out. . . .

"All we can do for now is follow the skull," he said. "The Professor will be guarding the last two pieces with all his might."

He swallowed the last of the seaweed cake, and called Rivet to him. Opening the storage compartment in the dogbot's back, he took out both pieces of the skull. "What now?" he asked.

Lia took them from him and held the two sections together, matching their cracked edges. A flash of blue light made Max cover his eyes, but it faded

quickly. When he looked again, the fragments of skull had become one, fused together without even a mark to show they were ever broken. The long jawbone jutted out beneath the powerful, staring brow. There was still a gaping hole in the middle of the face, and the top edges were broken.

"Thallos must have been a strange-looking creature," said Max.

Lia scowled at him, but her smile quickly returned. The faint blue glow seemed to shine from her skin for a moment. "I can feel it," she said. "The power is coming back."

Max could sense something, too, as if the water all around was filled with life. Even Spike was staring, hypnotized by the skull.

"Tell me more about Thallos," said Max.

Lia ran her hands over the smooth bone. "We have all sorts of legends, but nobody really knows much. He was an ancient creature, and a powerful one. Once the Merryn were wanderers — we traveled the seas in tribes. But the skull drew us together. By living close to it, we developed our powers."

Max thought back over all he'd learned since coming underwater. Before the Professor had struck, the Merryn had the ability to control the seas. Not using barriers and tide-breaks and fancy technology like the humans of Aquora City, but with the power of their minds. They could communicate with every living creature under the waves, and lived in peace.

The Professor had ruined that when he took the skull and broke it. Even though Max had gills now, he still felt a little ashamed to be a human — a Breather. He knew he'd do everything in his power to help recover the other skull pieces.

Lia released the skull and it turned in the water, directing them away from the coral reef.

"Let's go get the aquabike," Max said. "I can't keep getting lifts from Rivet."

They swam back out of the cavern through the narrow passage and found the bike floating in the water. A small octopus had wrapped its legs around the handlebars and lazily detached itself as they approached. Max checked the controls and fuel gauge. "Should be fine," he said, climbing into the saddle.

"We should rest first," said Lia. "There's a big ocean out there, with lots of dangers."

Max opened his mouth to argue, but a wave of weariness washed over him. He hadn't slept since he'd been in his bed on the 523rd floor of Tower Alpha Four; the place he'd once called home.

"You're right," he said. "But we can't sleep in the open. The Professor might send one of his creatures after us."

"I know just the thing," said Lia. "Follow me."

Max set the bike to CRUISE, and they traveled steeply downward, leveling off at the seabed. A carpet of bushy weeds rippled in the gentle current. Lia was scanning the way ahead and steered off to the left. The ground dipped away in a small crater, and at the bottom two giant spiral shells lay on their sides. Each was as big as an Aquora City transporter. The white edges of the shells curled away, perfectly smooth and speckled with pink flecks.

"Does anything *live* in there?" asked Max.

Lia shook her head. "Not anymore."

She leaped off Spike and folded herself into the shell's opening.

"Keep a lookout, Rivet," Max said.

He parked the aquabike beside the shell and climbed in. The surface felt strangely warm and soft and made a perfect bed.

It wasn't long before he could hear the soft rumble of Lia's snores. Spike lay beside her with his eyes half-closed. Max knew that he'd fall asleep soon, but his head was still buzzing with thoughts. Once, a year or so ago, he'd stood with his father, watching the fishing boats draw up at Aquora docks. One of the fishermen, an old man with a white beard and deep lines crossing his face, had shown them a shell he'd dredged up in his nets. It looked like the ones they slept in now, but smaller, about the size of a clenched fist.

"There you go, youngster," the fisherman had said, tossing the shell over. "A present for you. Close your eyes and hold it up to your ear."

Max's father had frowned, but nodded.

Max did as he was told, and pressed the cold shell against his ear. At once he'd heard an echoing, swirling sound, like crashing waves whipped by winds.

"Can you hear it?" the fisherman had asked. "The sound of the sea?"

Max smiled at the memory. He'd thought it was magic, those howling winds and the rush of water, trapped inside a tiny shell. His father had hated the sea ever since Max's mom disappeared, but he'd let Max listen to that sound.

Max turned over in his shell bed to make himself more comfortable, and listened to the sounds of the sea all around him. Rivet lay in the sand on the

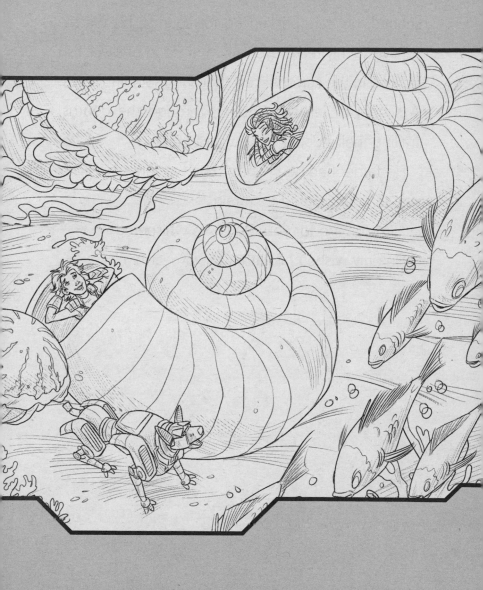

seabed, his ears pricked up for sounds, his watchful eyes dimly red. Beyond him, a cloud of silver fish danced in the current like a thousand spinning coins. A school of jellyfish bobbed through the depths, trailing their fluorescent purple bodies.

His father had been right to be fearful — but Max wouldn't let himself be afraid.

"I'm coming for you, Dad," he whispered.

He only wished his father could hear him.

DIVE INTO THE NEXT ADVENTURE!

DON'T MISS

DEEP DIVE #3: MANAK THE MANTA RAY

WE'D BETTER GET MOVING," MAX SAID WHEN they finished eating. They had to find the next piece of the Skull of Thallos, stolen by the evil Professor. Without the skull, the Merryn's aqua powers were fading, and Lia's people would not be able to defend themselves against the Professor's plans to enslave them all and rule the ocean. But Max also had his own reason for wanting to defeat the Professor. He'd kidnapped Max's dad.

"Did you have enough to eat?" Lia asked.

"Definitely," Max said.

He touched Rivet's head, and the robodog, who had been in sleep mode, instantly awoke. His stumpy robot tail wagged from side to side. "Morning, Max. Morning, girl. Morning, fish."

"Good boy, Rivet." Max opened the storage compartment in Rivet's back and got out the two-part piece of the Skull of Thallos that they had taken from the Robobeasts, Cephalox and Silda. The pieces had fused together, as though they had never been separated, to form the lower half of the skull. It glowed with a soft, steady blue light. Max looked at the pointed jaw and the gaping eye sockets and could hardly stop himself from shuddering.

He released the skull. It floated in the water in front of him, then slowly turned and held steady.

"To the North!" Lia said.

"How do you know that way's North?" Max asked. "There's no sun down here to get your bearings from."

"I'm Merryn," Lia said. "We always know where we are in the sea."

Max got on his aquabike and revved the engine. Rivet paddled over to his side, and Max returned the skull to Rivet's back compartment. Lia sat astride Spike and led the way out of the cave.

Soon they were cruising through the ocean at top speed. They didn't speak much as they raced over undersea hills and valleys, past shoals of fish and fields of gently waving seaweed. Max was thinking about the clue they had found in the Professor's abandoned submarine — was it only yesterday? They now knew that the Professor's base was the Black Caves. And that must be where Max's dad was being held. But where in all the oceans of Nemos could the Black Caves be?

"Wait!" Lia said. She touched Spike's side to slow him down. Max hit the brakes.

"What?"

Lia looked worried. "If we keep going North, we'll reach the Forest of Souls."

"Is that bad?" Max asked.

"We mustn't go there unprepared!" Lia said.

Abruptly, she swung Spike around and headed off to the side.

"Where are you going?" called Max.

Lia shouted something over her shoulder, but Max couldn't hear.

He twisted the throttle and raced to catch up with

her. There was only one thought in his head now. *What is the Forest of Souls?*

Max saw Lia and Spike stop beside a huge black rock. He eased the aquabike to a halt by their side.

"What are you doing?" he asked.

"Watch." Lia made a piercing, whistling sound from the back of her throat. For a second, nothing happened. Then a host of little golden gleams of light shot out from cracks in the boulder — thousands of them, dancing around Max and Lia in a glittering swarm.

Max saw that they were tiny fish. Each was no longer than the joint of a finger, and they glowed different shades, some gold, some orange, some copper, some yellow, some almost white. He and Lia were standing in a sphere of shifting light. The sparkles were reflected in Rivet's metal sides, and the sand on the ocean floor shone brilliant silver.

"Wow," Max said softly. "That's incredible."

Lia seemed pleased. "They're pretty, aren't they? They're called glindles."

"They're beautiful," Max said. "Thanks for showing them to me — only, do we have time for this? I mean, we're on a mission here."

"They'll light our way through the Forest of Souls," Lia said.

"Isn't there a danger that these . . . glindles will attract predators?"

Lia shook her head. "Absolutely not. Glindles give off a scent that repels other sea creatures. They will light the way and keep us safe from the creatures that lurk in the Forest of Souls."

Max felt a twinge of unease. "What creatures?"

"No one knows for sure," Lia said in a low voice, as if she feared someone was listening. "There are only rumors — legends. But it is said that dangerous monsters dwell there."

Max began to wonder if they would need something more than fish scent to get them safely through.

Lia made the whistling noise again, and the glindles followed her in a gleaming crowd as she steered Spike back toward the north.

Max rode beside her, enjoying the sensation of moving in a bubble of light. From time to time, Lia took scraps of kelp or fungus from her tunic and gave it to the glindles to nibble. Spike turned to look at her reproachfully, and she fed him, too.

After a time, Max saw that Rivet was struggling — the poor dogbot wasn't built to keep up with Spike or the aquabike.

"Here, Rivet!" Max patted the space at the back of the bike. Rivet wagged his stumpy tail and jumped up behind Max. He sat there, resting his propellers, as they rode farther and farther north.

Eventually, the scenery began to change. The dark green seaweed that was dotting the ocean bed began to grow more thickly. The fronds grew taller — huge feathery arms that swayed in the ocean currents like the branches of trees in a breeze. Max began to feel hemmed in by the forest of dark, slimy seaweed that surrounded them, soaring far above their heads. If it hadn't been for the glindles, they would hardly have been able to see a thing.

"Is this it?" Max said. "The Forest of Souls?"

Lia inclined her head. "It is the beginning."

"Then let's check our location," Max said.

Max reached behind him and took out the Skull of Thallos from Rivet's storage compartment. He held it in front of him, and frowned. Something was wrong. The skull wasn't glowing as steadily as before. Its light pulsed weakly, faded away, then flared up briefly before fading away again.

He let go of it, watching to see where it pointed. But the skull just bobbed in the water in front of him, slowly turning around, not settling on any direction.

"It's not working anymore!" Max groaned. "Is that because we're in the Forest of Souls?"

"It must be," Lia said in that same hushed voice she'd used earlier. "We must be very, very careful. No Merryn would enter this forest willingly."

Max felt like saying, *Neither would I*, but stopped himself. If he wanted to be brave, he had to sound brave. "It'll be fine," he said. "We know we're going in the right direction, and as long as we stick together we're bound to find some clue. If the Robobeast is hiding in here, we'll find it. We have the glindles, don't we?"

Lia nodded slowly. She patted Spike and they moved on. The fronds of seaweed became even thicker, pressing in on them.

Then, suddenly, they emerged into a clearing. Lia was ahead and Max heard her cry out in alarm. "Max!"

The next moment his own stomach twisted with fear.

Standing in the clearing, as if awaiting their arrival, was a green creature, the size of a man. There were frills around its lizard-like head. Beady black eyes stared straight at them and its mouth was twisted in an evil grin.

Max tensed. *This must be one of the creatures that live here,* he thought. *And if I have to fight my way past it . . . bring it on!*

BEASTQUEST®

→ THE DARK REALM ←

BEASTQUEST®
AMULET OF AVANTIA
NIXA THE DEATH BRINGER
SCHOLASTIC

BEASTQUEST®
AMULET OF AVANTIA
EQUINUS THE SPIRIT HORSE
SCHOLASTIC

BEASTQUEST®
AMULET OF AVANTIA
RASHOUK THE CAVE TROLL
SCHOLASTIC

FIGHT THE BEASTS

BEASTQUEST®
AMULET OF AVANTIA
LUNA THE MOON WOLF
SCHOLASTIC

BEASTQUEST®
AMULET OF AVANTIA
BLAZE THE ICE DRAGON
SCHOLASTIC

BEASTQUEST®
AMULET OF AVANTIA
STEALTH THE GHOST PANTHER
SCHOLASTIC

FEAR THE MAGIC